THE **Fang**

WRITTEN, ILLUSTRATED and DESIGNED BY MARC J PALMI

self
SATISFIED

THE FANG - VOLUME 2 WEEKEND AT MEDUSA'S

A SELF SATISFIED BOOK COPYRIGHT MARC J PALM 2021

FIRST PRINTING 2021

ISBN: 978-1-68396-494-0

CONTENTS

GUTTER PUNK ALLEY RAT

Chapter 1

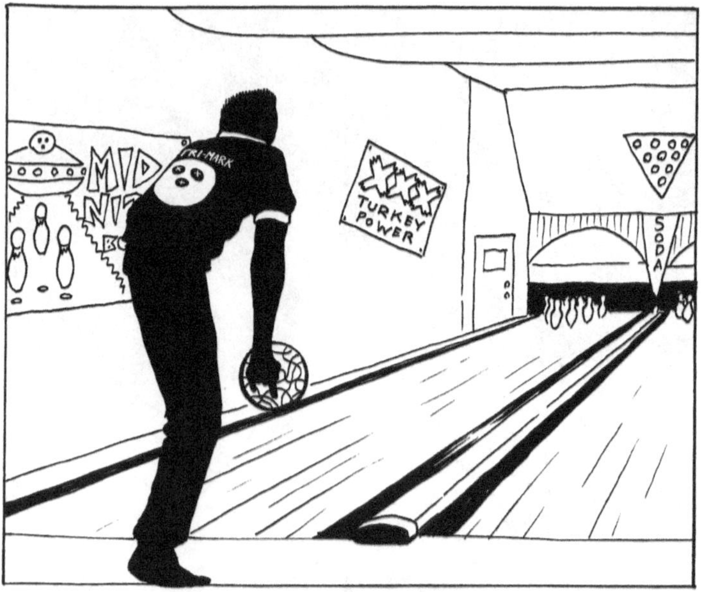
MID
TRI-MARK
XXX
TURKEY POWER
SODA

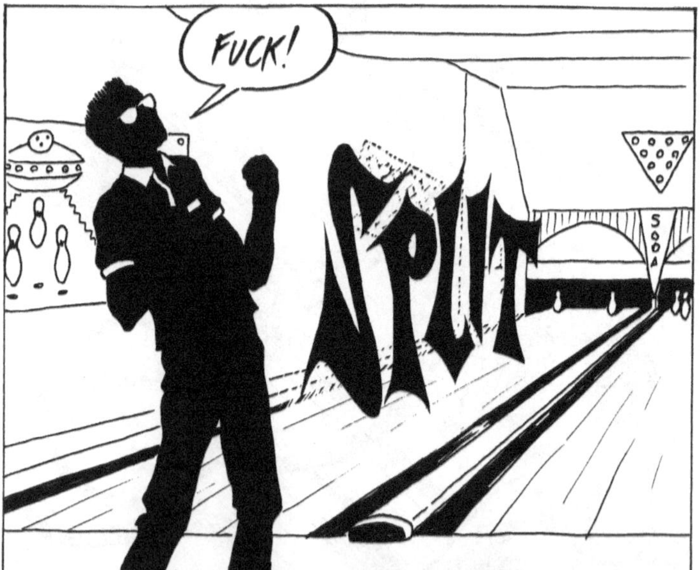
FUCK!
SPLIT
SODA

EMPLOYEES ONLY
DA

EMPLOYEES ONLY
DA
SQUEEK
GURGLE GURGLE
DAMN IT! MY BALL MUST BE STUCK.

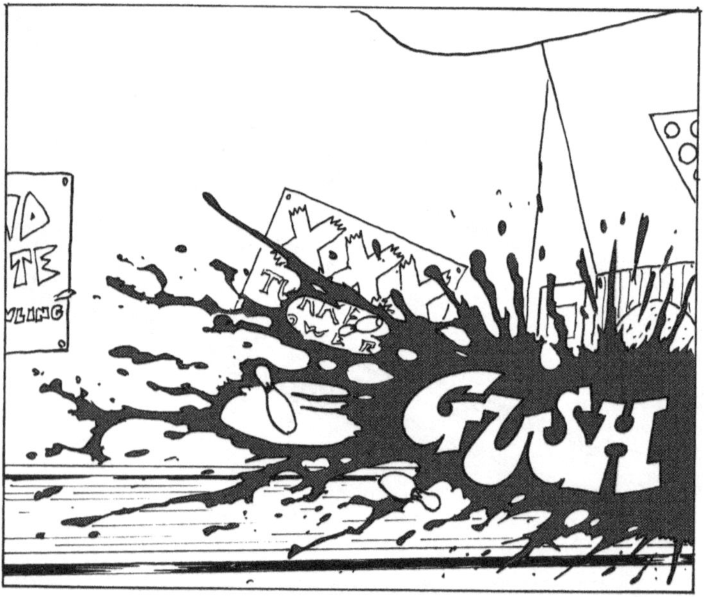
GUSH

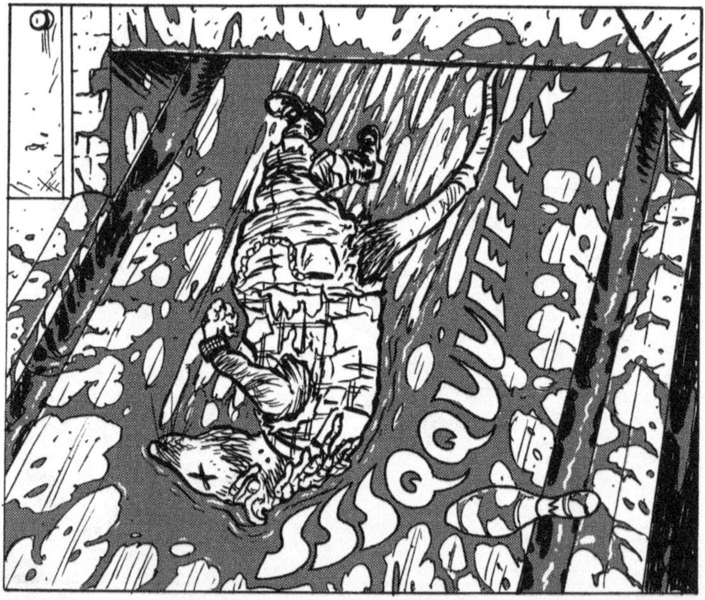
SSQQUEEEK

KEEP CLOSED
RATSTIN' FRATSTIN'...

BLEECH! YOU TASTE LIKE THE SEWAGE YOU LIVED IN.
HELP!
DUCKY WUZ
BLECH
SLOPPY M-BOPPY

I JUST NEED YOU TO SAY "CHEESE" FOR THE CLIENT.
THEN I'M GETTING OUT OF HERE!

WHAT THE FUCK IS IN YOUR MOUTH?!
MAGNIFICATION X50

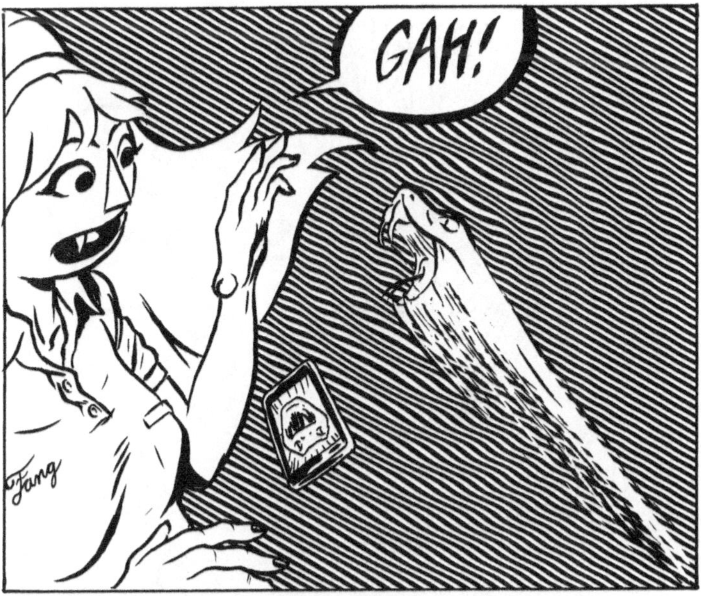
GAH!
Fang

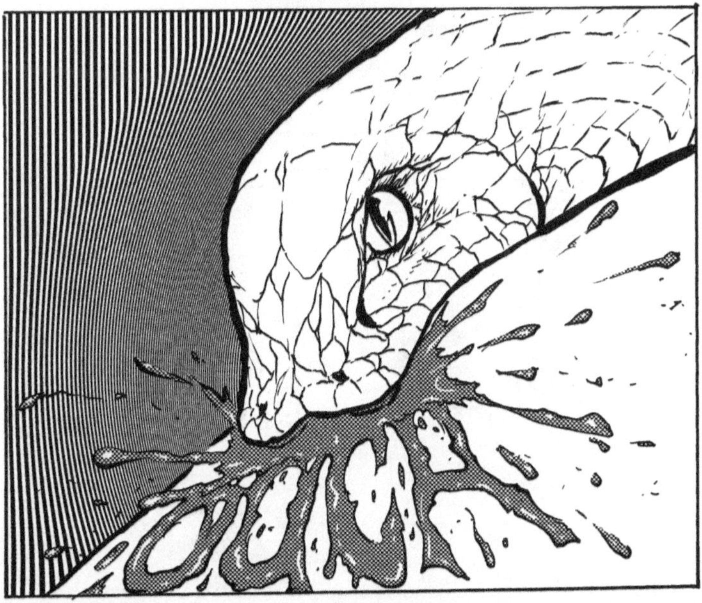

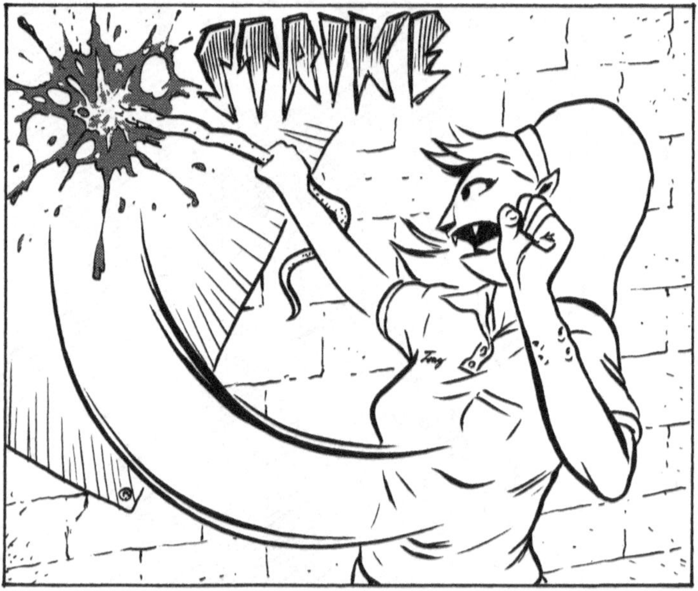
STRIKE

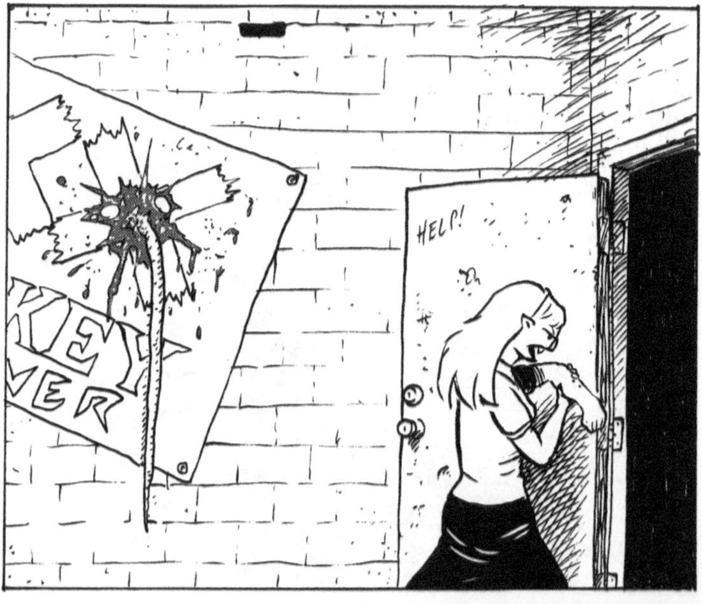
HELP!

VENOM

Chapter
2

I WOULD NOT HAVE MADE IT HOME.

THE VENOM HAD BROUGHT ON A MAJOR "TRIP".

I GOT TO **ONE OF MY** SAFE HOUSES.

AND **TRIPPED BALLS** ALL NIGHT TIL DAWN.

I HAVE AN ITCHY FEELING THAT THIS IS A MESSAGE FROM MEDUSA!
I ♡
22 oz
THAT ALWAYS WORKS

YEEEAAH... HEH HEH... THAT SOUNDS LIKE HER STYLE.

IS THIS A KISS OF DEATH!? AM I MARKED?!
I ♡ BLOOD
12oz

WE WOULDN'T BE HERE TALKING IF SHE WANTED YOU DEAD.
IT COULD BE A WARNING.

THE SSSORCCERESSS ISSS SSUMMONING YOU.
SMOKE?

GAH!! WHAT THE SHIT!? NO!!

IS THIS HOW SHE COMMONLY COMMUNICATES? "SNAKE-BITE-O-GRAM"?
HAH HAH HAH!!
SORRY.
NO...
WELL... KIND OF... WHEN SHE'S PISSED OFF.
I HELPED OUT THIS ONE GAL I KNEW. SHE WAS ALWAYS GETTING HARASSED.

(insert inappropriate comment here)

SO I HOOK HER UP WITH A SPELL THAT WILL *TEMPORARILY* TURN SOMEONE TO STONE WITH A LOOK.

SHE **REALLY** GOT **INTO IT!**
STARTED **PUSHING** WHAT SHE
WORE, **FURTHER** AND **FURTHER.**

DIRT-BAGS WERE GETTING
STONED, LEFT AND RIGHT.

SHE GOT SLOPPY THOUGH. **REALLY ABUSING THE
POWER.** GETTING A LOT OF EYES ON HER IN
WAYS THAT THE **REAL MEDUSA** WAS
NOT AMUSED BY.

MEDUSA REACHED OUT SOON AFTER THAT.

SHE ENDED UP PARALYZED IN HER BED FOR A WEEK, FROM ALL OF THE SNAKE BITES.

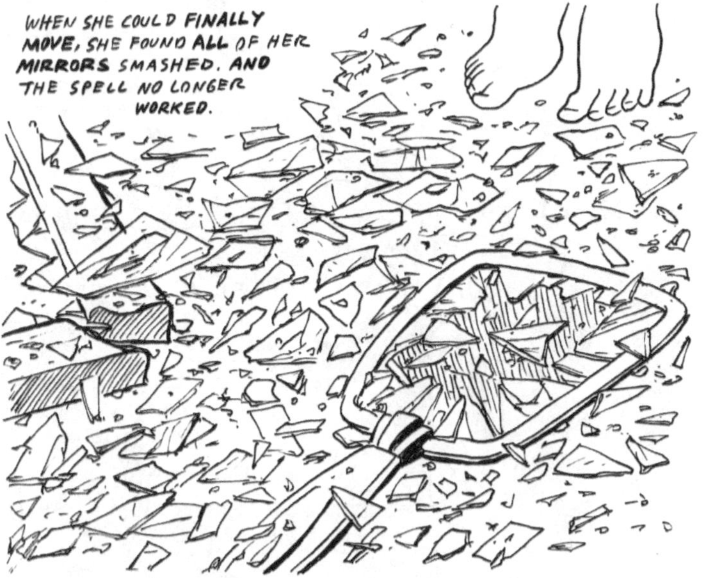

WHEN SHE COULD **FINALLY** MOVE, SHE FOUND **ALL** OF HER **MIRRORS** SMASHED. AND THE SPELL NO LONGER WORKED.

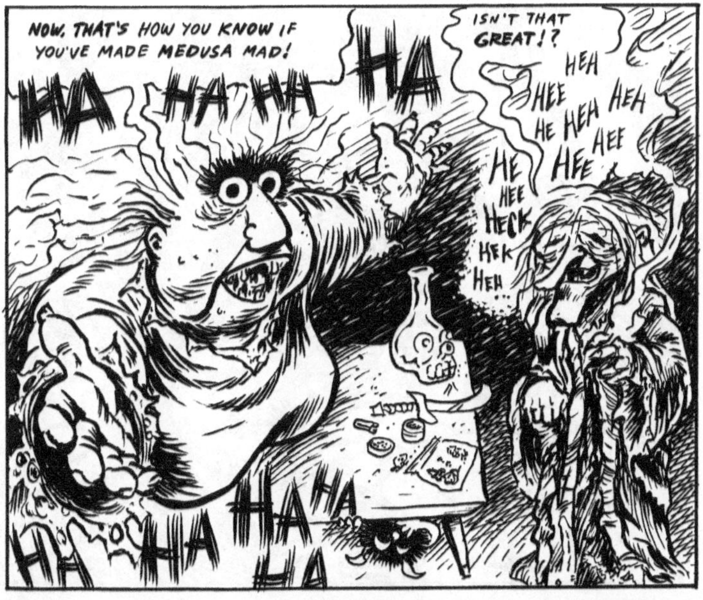

NOW, **THAT'S** HOW YOU KNOW IF YOU'VE MADE MEDUSA MAD!

ISN'T THAT **GREAT!?**

HA HA HA HA

HEH HEE HE HEA HEH AEF HE HEE HE

HE HEE HECK HEK HEH

HA HA HA HA HA

UUHH... THAT DOESN'T REALLY SOOTHE MY NERVES.
HOLD YOUR HORSES!
LET'S TAKE A LOOK IN THE CRYSTAL AND SEE WHAT WE CAN, UM..?
WELL...
SEE!

STRANGE!
oOH YEAH... THAT'S REALLY WEIRD!

SHE SEEMS TO BE **SPLIT**. AS IF SHE'S IN **DIFFERENT** PLACES AT **ONCE**.

IT'S **REALLY UNCLEAR WHERE** YOU WILL **FIND** HER. WE **THINK** SHE'S AT **ONE** OF **TWO** HOUSES.

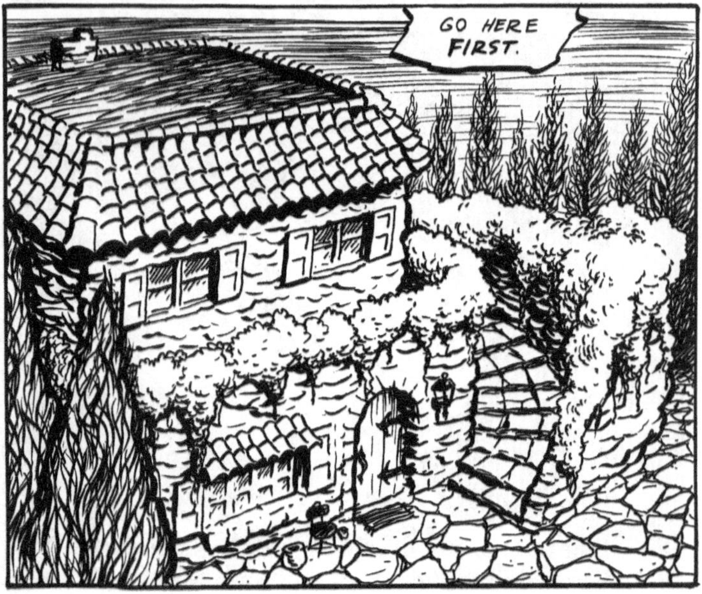
GO HERE FIRST.

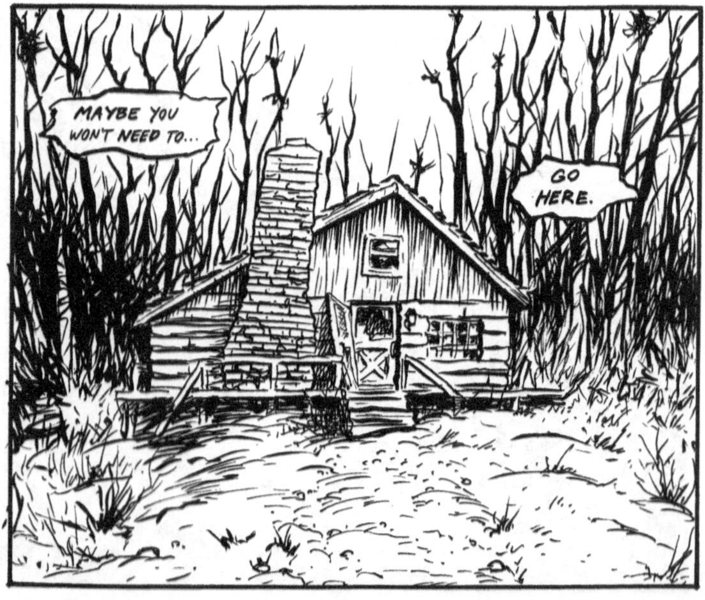
MAYBE YOU WON'T NEED TO...
GO HERE.

FANG!? IS THAT YOU WITH THAT CUTE HAT? IN THIS MIRROR, I CAN ONLY SEE YOUR CLOTHES.

UH... YEAH. HI! SORRY.

YOU SEE, WITHOUT THIS MIRROR I'D GET YOU MORE STONED THAN THOSE WITCHES COULD!

HEH MAYBE...

HAVE A SEAT.

EH...

WOW! THAT'S AWESOME!

I'M HAPPY TO HAVE THE INFAMOUS "MONSTER HUNTER" IN MY HOME. I'M *CURIOUS* WHY YOU'VE COME TO VISIT? CONSIDERING MY *HISTORY* WITH *THOSE WITCH* FRIENDS OF YOURS, THAT IS...

THERE **USED** TO BE **THREE** WITCHES, **RIGHT?**

MAYBE? THAT'S BEFORE MY TIME.

AH HA! THAT'S RIGHT, YOU'RE A RELATIVELY YOUNG VAMPIRE.

HEH... **YEAH** "RELATIVELY".

SO, IF **YOU** DIDN'T **INVITE** ME HERE...

THEN DO YOU **KNOW** WHO **COULD** HAVE SENT ME A "**STINGING TELEGRAM**"?

I'D LIKE TO KNOW MYSELF! YOU KNOW, MY NAME AND REPUTATION GETS MISUSED, MISREPRESENTED AND MISTAKEN! THEN I GET ALL THE HEAT!
PEOPLE USE CHEAP MAGIC TO IMITATE ME FOR THEIR OWN BENEFIT. SOME HAVE USED MY OLD SKINS FOR VARIOUS CAPERS.

OLD SKINS?
I HAVE TO MOLT MY SKIN EVERY DECADE. KEEPS ME LOOKING GOOD! THAT'S WHY THEY SAY- "SCALES DON'T FAIL."

OK, I'M SORRY TO BOTHER YOU THEN. I HAVE ANOTHER LEAD...

DON'T RUSH OUT THE DOOR YET, "MONSTER KILLER"! SINCE YOU'RE HERE, I REQUIRE YOUR SERVICES.

NOW YOU SEE, I'M SICK AS SPIT ABOUT MY NAME AND STORY BEING EXPLOITED! I DON'T WANT TO BE RESPONSIBLE FOR SOME IMITATOR'S SHIT!

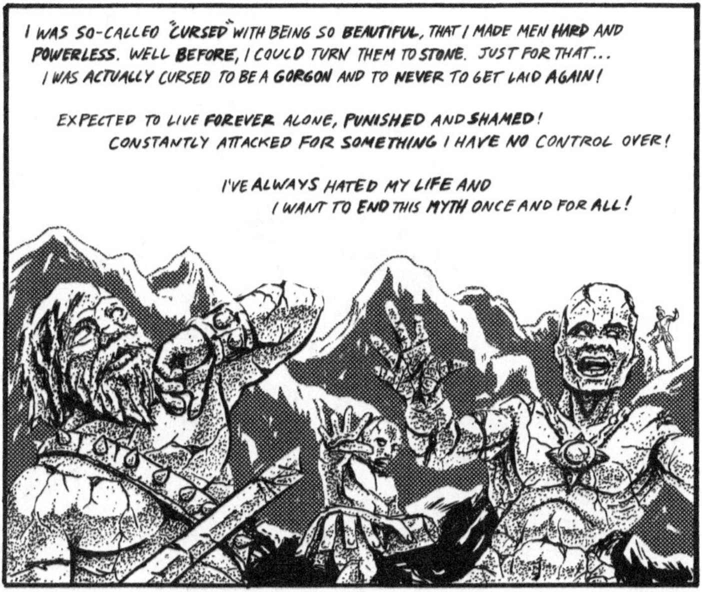

I WAS SO-CALLED "CURSED" WITH BEING SO **BEAUTIFUL**, THAT I MADE MEN **HARD** AND **POWERLESS**. WELL **BEFORE**, I COULD TURN THEM TO STONE. JUST FOR THAT... I WAS ACTUALLY CURSED TO BE A **GORGON** AND TO NEVER TO GET LAID **AGAIN**!

EXPECTED TO LIVE **FOREVER** ALONE, **PUNISHED** AND **SHAMED**! CONSTANTLY ATTACKED FOR **SOMETHING** I HAVE NO CONTROL OVER!

I'VE **ALWAYS** HATED MY **LIFE** AND I WANT TO **END** THIS **MYTH** ONCE AND FOR ALL!

I WANT TO **END MY LIFE**! WITHOUT ME, IT'LL BE EASIER TO KNOW WHO THE **BOOTLEGGERS** ARE OUT THERE. **NO ONE** NEEDS TO BE LIKE ME!

YOU **GOT** TO END THEM FOR ME FANG. I MEAN, WHY CAN'T **YOU** REPRESENT THE NEXT WAVE OF **POWERFUL** AND **INTELLIGENT** WOMEN? I'LL GET OUT OF YOUR WAY SO THAT YOU CAN **SHINE**.

IT WAS **VERY** FORTUITOUS THAT *YOU* **ENDED** UP HERE FANG. YOU ARE THE **PERFECT** PERSON TO DO THIS.
YOU **NEED** TO CUT *MY* **HEAD OFF NOW**!!

WHAT THE....!?

I'M **NO** PERSEUS! I CAN'T KILL YOU.

A SECOND AGO, I SAID YOU WERE A "POWERFUL", "INTELLIGENT" WOMAN.
DON'T LET ME DOWN NOW!!
ALSO... FUCK PERSEUS!!

WHOA, CHAIR!

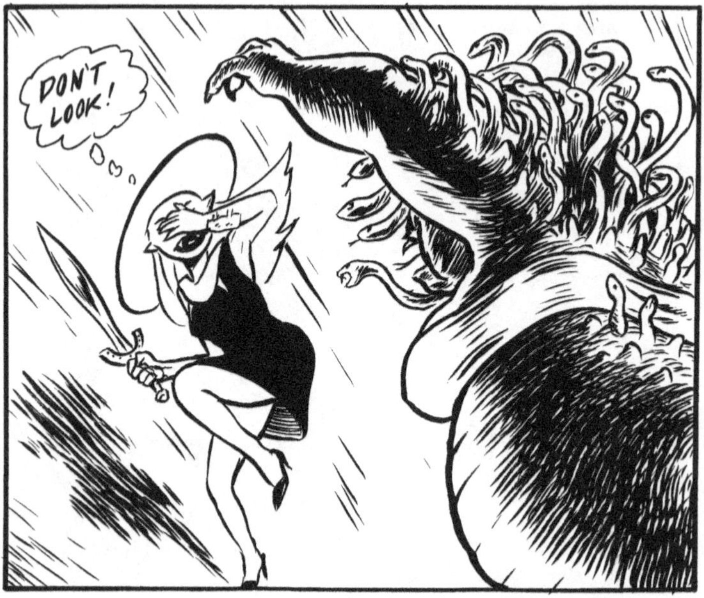
DON'T LOOK!

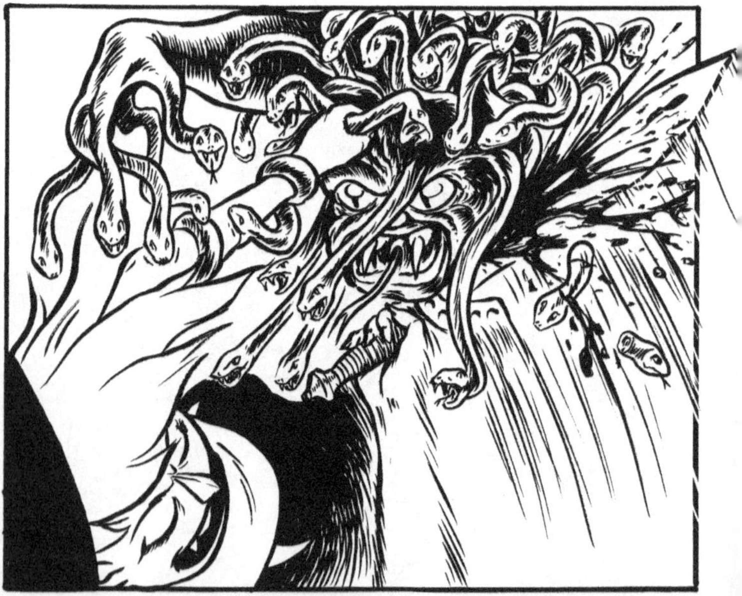

WHO AUTHORIZED THE HIT ON MEDUSA?

OH SHIT...

IT WAS **NOT** A HIT! SHE WAS IN A **BAD PLACE.**
DEPRESSED AND TALKING ABOUT **ENDING HER LIFE.**
SHE **THREW** A SWORD AT ME AND THEN **ATTACKED.**
I **HAD** TO **DEFEND** MYSELF.

SHIT!

THE **GROUP** THINKS IT WAS AN **UNAUTHORIZED** HIT. THEY'RE **PISSED!** THEY **SUSPECT** YOU MIGHT BE **GUNNING** FOR **ANOTHER** COMPANY. YOU BETTER COME IN **WILLFULLY**... AND TALK. YOU **NEED** TO BRING **EVIDENCE** TO SUPPORT YOUR CASE.

SHIIIITT...

OH! I'LL HAVE SOME **SOLID** EVIDENCE!

BE ON GUARD OUT THERE.

SHIT YEAH.

41

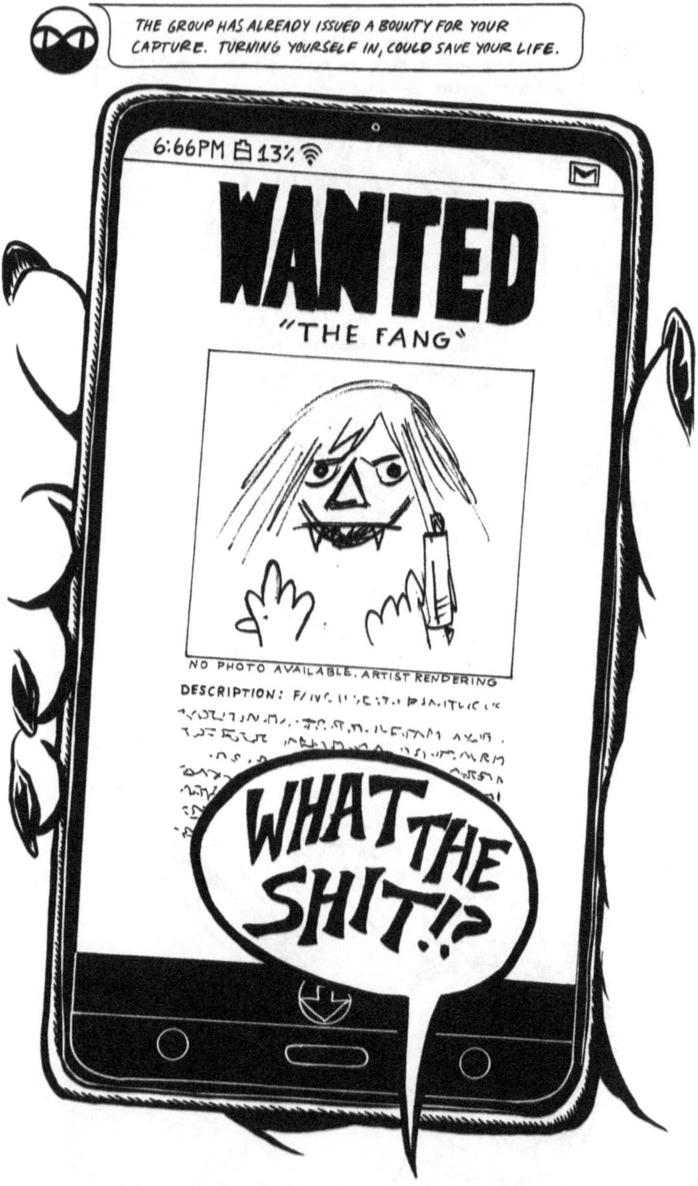

THE GROUP HAS ALREADY ISSUED A BOUNTY FOR YOUR CAPTURE. TURNING YOURSELF IN, COULD SAVE YOUR LIFE.

ARE YOU **SERIOUS**?!
THAT DRAWING LOOKS **SO** AMATURE!

THIS **IS** SERIOUS.

SHITTY!

I KNOW I'M HARD TO **PHOTOGRAPH** BUT, **C'MON**...
THERE'S **BETTER** FAN ART OUT THERE!

DON'T SAY I **DIDN'T** WARN YOU.

THIS IS THE **SHIT** I'M TALKING ABOUT.

WEEKEND AT MEDUSA'S

Chapter 5

I KIND OF FIGURED I'D END UP HERE.

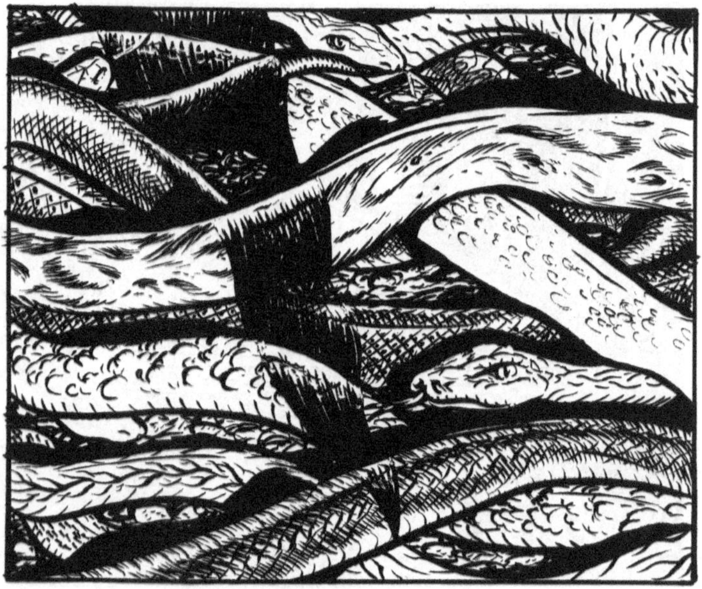

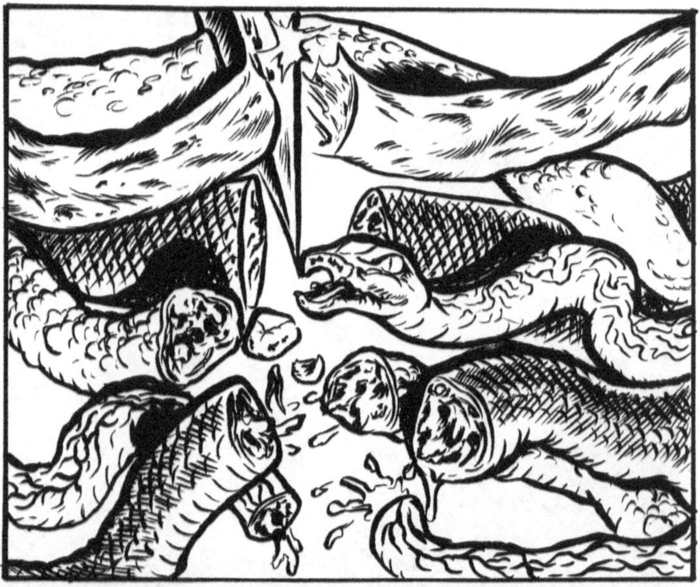

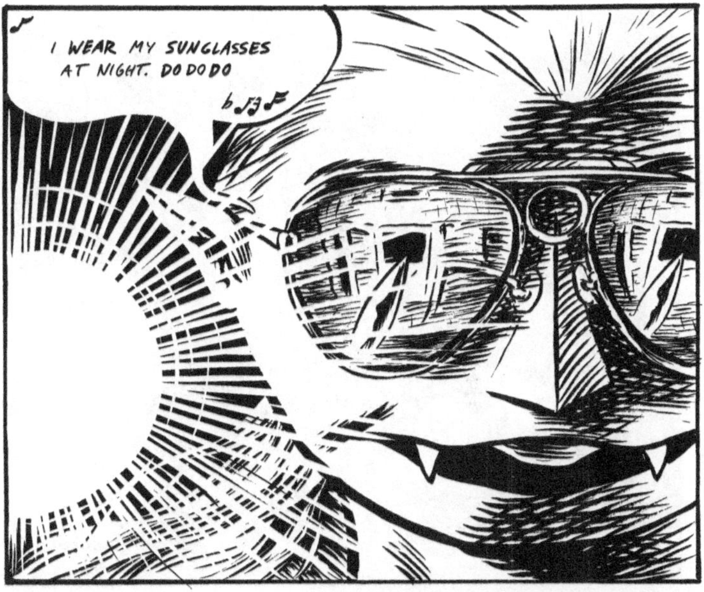
I WEAR MY SUNGLASSES AT NIGHT. DODODO

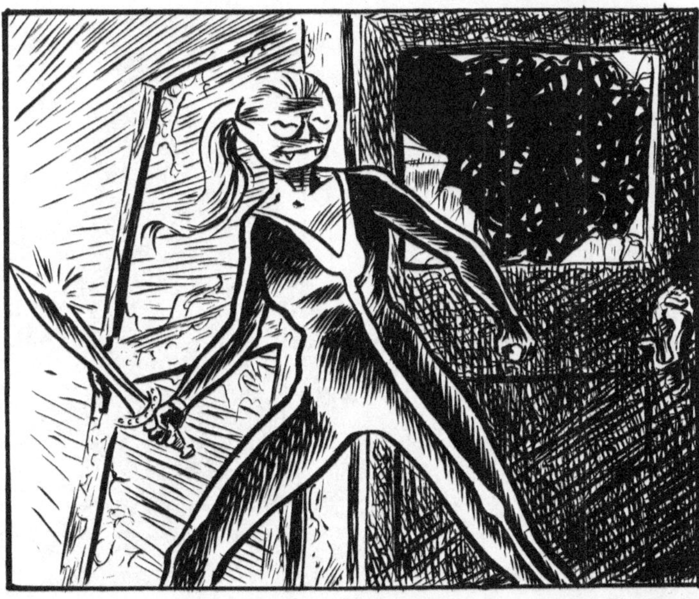

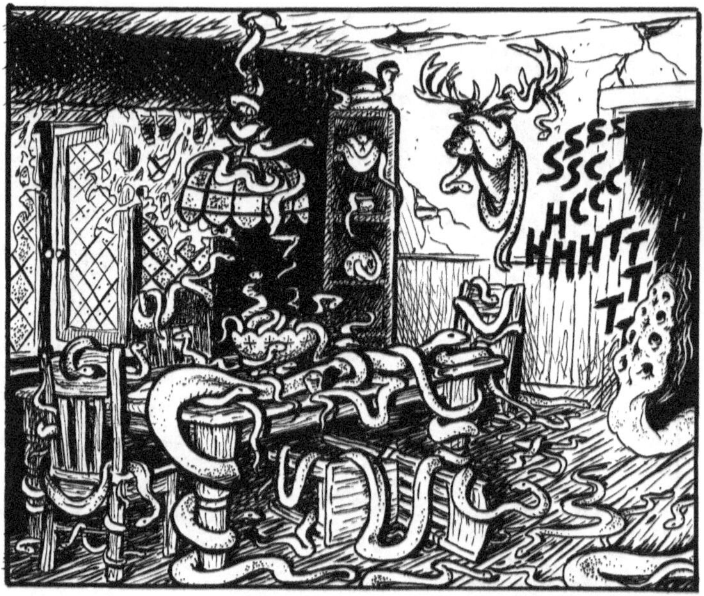
SSSS
SSCCC
HCCC
HHHHTT
TT
TT

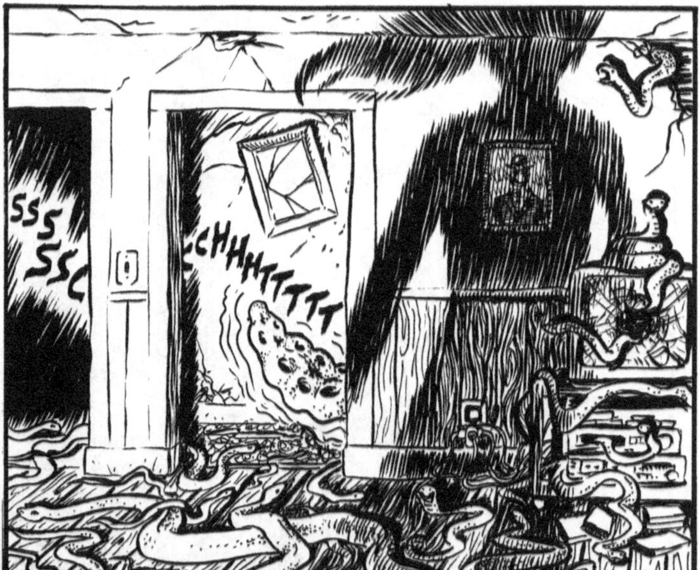
SSS
SSC
CCHHHHTTTTTT

OH HI! I HOPE I DIDN'T SCARE YOU. I JUST LET MYSELF IN.

SSSHHEE LIED TO YOOUU.
I TRIED TO WARN YOU.
SSSHHH

WHY WOULD YOU DO SOMETHING LIKE THAT?

HER DEATH WASSSS NOT ABOUT ENDING THINGSSSS.

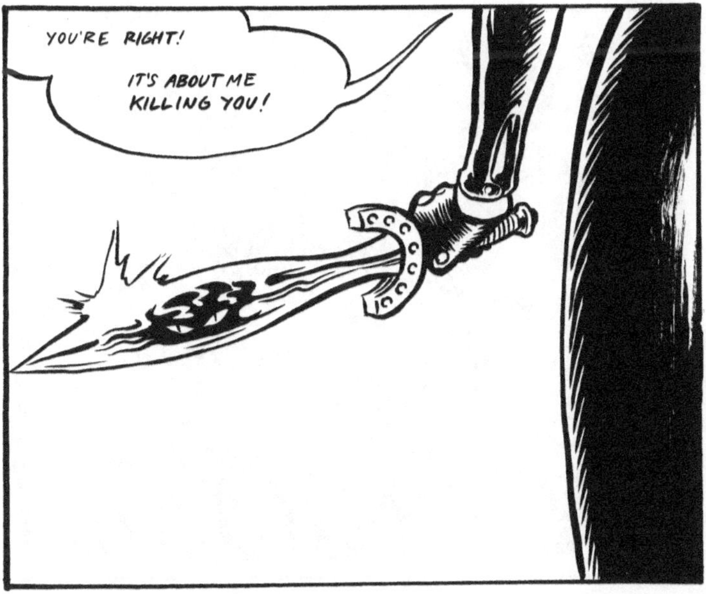
YOU'RE RIGHT!
IT'S ABOUT ME KILLING YOU!

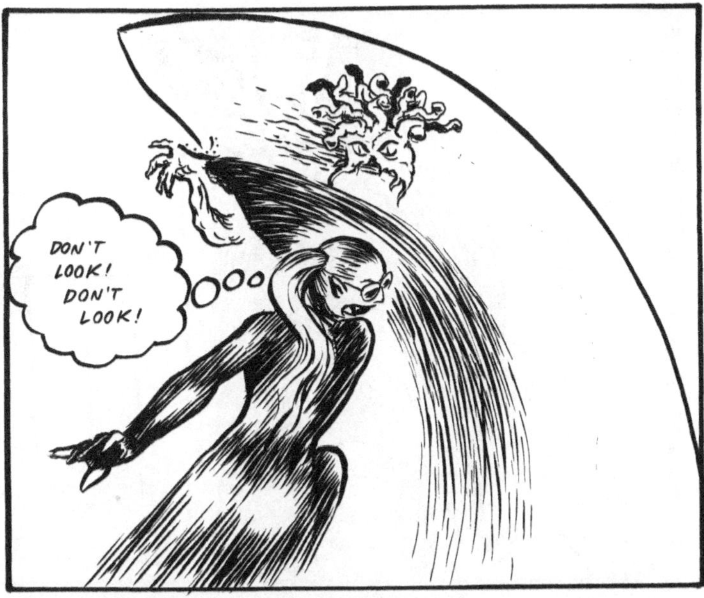
DON'T LOOK! DON'T LOOK!

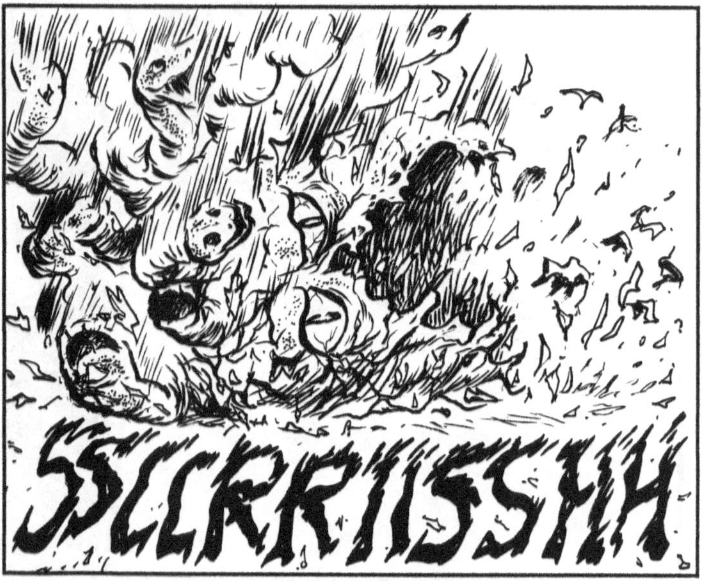
SSCRRIISSHH

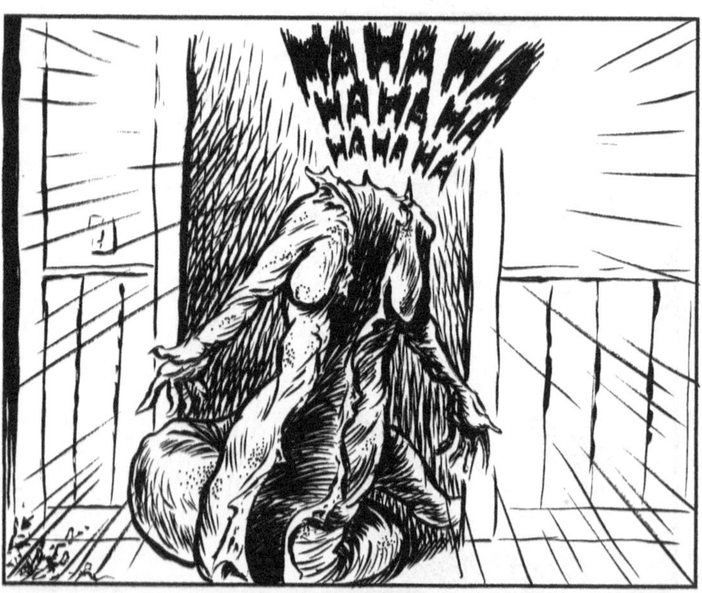
HAHAHA
HAHAHA
HAHAHAHA

SHIT...

HA! HA! HA!!! YOU CAN'T KILL ME!!!
I'M A DEMON!! WEARIN' SOME KILLER THREADS, RIGHT?

I CAN SEE YOU DON'T LIKE TO FUCK AROUND. I'LL CUT OUT THIS HORROR MOVIE SHIT AND WE CAN TALK DEMON TO DEMON, OR WHATEVER YOU ARE.

MEDUSA IS MANIPULATING YOU! SHE WANTS TO DEFLECT ANY HEAT SHE GETS ONTO SOMEONE ELSE. IF YOU BECOME THE ONE PEOPLE WANT TO MAKE LEGENDS OUT OF, THEN SHE CAN KEEP DOING THINGS BEHIND THE SCENES.

ALOT OF THIS HAS TO DO WITH THOSE WITCHES TOO. SHE WANTS TO GET TO THEM THROUGH YOU.

HOW DO YOU FIT IN?!

HEH HEH HEH

I DON'T FIT IN! I'M JUST HERE TO STIR SHIT UP.

DEMONS ARE AGENTS OF **CHAOS!** I'M NOT FAVORING ANY OUTCOME. I JUST LIKE TO PUSH BUTTONS!

YOU PRICK!

YOU SAID I CANNOT KILL YOU? EVEN IF I CHOP YOU INTO LITTLE PIECES?

THAT WOULD BE TOTALLY USELESS.

IT MIGHT HELP ME FEEL BETTER.

CATHARSIS
OH!
I HAVE NOTHING TO DO WITH THE WITCHES PAST. WHY RUIN MY LIFE?!
OUCH! ARE YOU ACTUALLY TALKING TO ME?

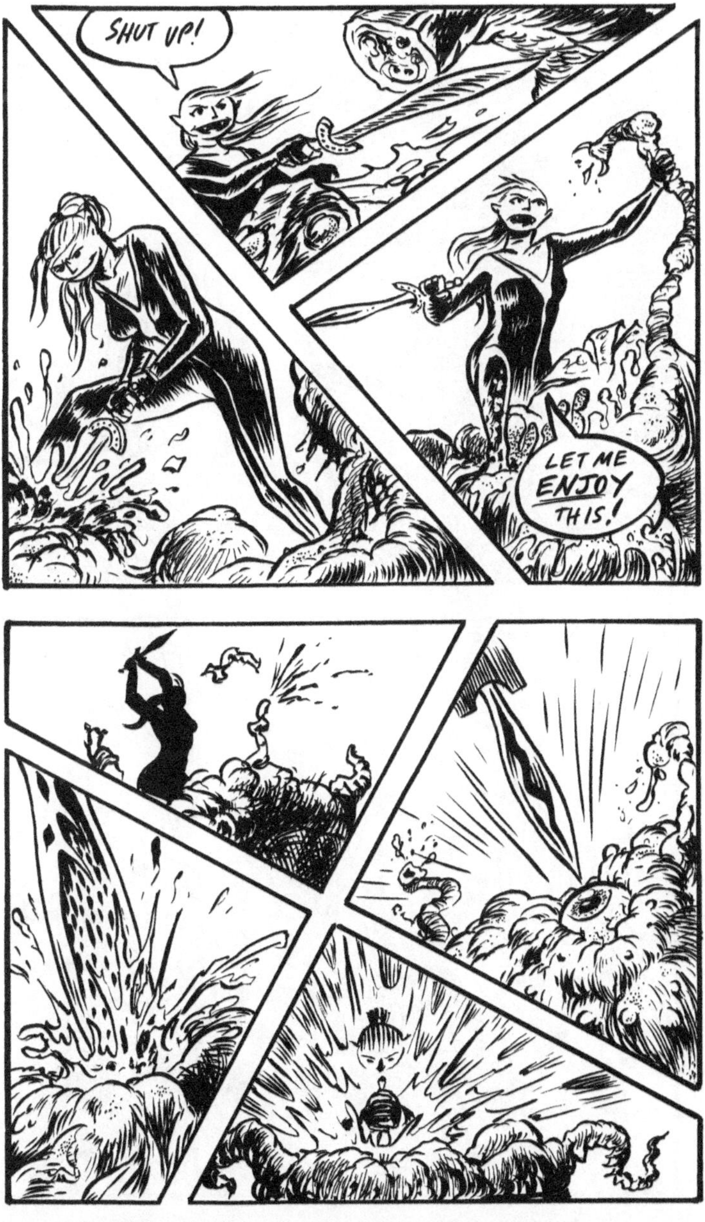
SHUT UP!
LET ME ENJOY THIS!

FEEL ANY BETTER?

NO! ;HUFF; I'M JUST EXHAUSTED. ;HUFF; I REALLY WISH I COULD KILL YOU!!

I'LL BET... THERE ARE GOIN' TO BE SOME BOUNTY HUNTERS SAYIN' THAT ABOUT YOU SOON.

FUCK YOU!

IF IT WAS A SNAKE

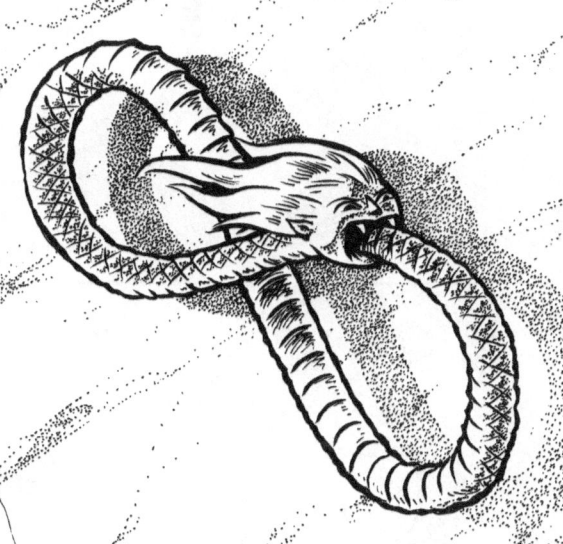

IT WOULD HAVE
BIT YOU

SO... EVEN IF, I WALKED IN WITH THE SWORD AND MEDUSA'S HEAD UNDER MY ARM... MY CAREER IS OVER!
IF I TRY AND RUN, THEY'D TORTURE YOU TWO FOR INFORMATION. THEN THEY WOULD TRY AND KILL ME. IF THEY FOUND OUT HOW.
I NEED TO KEEP THE TWO OF YOU ALIVE FOR MY OWN SELFISH REASONS.
UUUGGG
FWOMP
IMMORTALITY IS OVERRATED

YOU KNOW THERE ARE STORES THAT SELL WEED? YOU DON'T NEED TO ONLY COME HERE TO GET HIGH.
HEE HEE HEE
HA!

AS IF THAT WAS ALL YOU DID FOR ME.
YOU KNOW ME... I JUST WANT TO HAVE FUN.
I'M JUST SAYIN', THINGS MIGHT GET STRESSFUL. I DON'T LIKE STRESS. I DON'T DO WELL UNDER STRESS.
IMMORTALITY IS OVERRATED

WHOA!!
WHAT ARE YOU DOING? PUT THAT SHIT AWAY!

IT'S COOL, SHE'S GOT SHADES.

OH, RELAX... THAT THING IS HARMLESS.

THAT IS NOT ACTUALLY MEDUSA'S HEAD. THE FANG DIDN'T REALLY KILL HER.

HHMMPH... THAT'S DISAPPOINTING.

WAIT! SO THIS IS JUST ANOTHER ONE OF HER SKINS?

YUP!

NOW I WANT TO KILL HER! SHE'S GOING TO BE BREATHING DOWN MY NECK, FUCKING UP MY LIFE! OUR LIVES.

MEANWHILE...

ANY DICK WHO'S SEEN THAT **DUMB** POSTER WILL BE AFTER ME.

I AM **FULLY** AWARE OF HOW SHE CAN FUCK UP **OUR** LIVES. SHE IS **RESPONSIBLE** FOR **KILLING OUR SISTER.** YEARS BEFORE YOU ARRIVED!

YOU'RE GOING TO BE REALLY SURPRISED BY **HOW** POWERFUL SHE ACTUALLY IS.

LOOKING OVER MY SHOULDER IS NOTHING **NEW** TO ME.

MAYBE YOU'VE FORGOTTEN WHAT THAT FEELS LIKE.

"MONSTER-HUNTER."

IMMORTALITY

END?

BUY THIS STUFF BEFORE YOU DIE!

60 Pages

THE Fang

MOON LIGHT SNACK!

$7.99

Marc Palm introduces you to The Fang - the Monster Hunter and her world of... VAMPIRISM, LYCANTHROPY, ASSASSINATION, WITCHCRAFT, MARIJUANA and PERVERSION! Fang vol 1 - Moon Light Snack! 60 pg b/w pocketbook 4.25x6.25 full color cover.

Represent The **Monster Hunter** on your water bottle or trapper keeper and ward off fantastical ghastly creatures or real human monsters.

LIMITED EDITION 3 Sticker pack SUPPLY NEARLY DRAINED!!!

The Weed Witch and Hash Hag are there when you are in need. They'll always be around to cast laugh spells on you using special herbs!

Full color die-cut 3" inch sticker made out of weather proof vinyl

TOO CUTE!

ORDERING INFORMATION!!!

Fang vol 1 - Moon Light Snack $7.99
Fang 3 x Sticker pack $5.00
Weed Witch 3" sticker $3.00
Hash Hag 3" sticker $3.00
W.W. & H.H. sticker set $5.00

LIMITED-TIME FREE GIFT OFFER!

BUY DIRECT: etsy.com/shop/swellzombie
FAN CLUB: patreon.com/marcpalm

67

Fang Fan-art Contest Winners!! These pieces are featured on bottom of page 43.
This page - Nate McDonough, Brandon Lehmann, Jasper Jubenvill

This page - Robb Mirsky, JT Wilkins, Eric Priestly

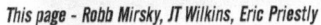

Copyright 2021 each individual artist

THANK YOU!!!

I appreciate the patience of those who
have waited for this volume to be released.
Your continued interest has been immensely helpful.
This is extended to my Patreon Patrons for their support.
The fans who contributed artwork to this book and the
Marks of the Fang fan zine! I have some insanely talented fans!!

Shout out to all the super important retailers who carry my books,
festival folk who I hope to see again, podcasters who had me as a
guest and my own online customers.

Special thanks to Rachel Leblanc for editorial assistance
and inspiration. Extra thank you Paul Constant,
Chris Esty, Larry Reid, Fantagraphics Books
& all BADASS women everywhere!